This book is your passport into time.

Can you survive World War I? Turn the page to find out.

Bantam Books in the Time Machine Series
Ask your bookseller for the books you have missed

#1 SECRET OF THE KNIGHTS
Jim Gasperini/illustrated by Richard Hescox

#2 SEARCH FOR DINOSAURS
David Bischoff/illustrated by Doug Henderson
and Alex Nino

#3 SWORD OF THE SAMURAI
Michael Reaves and Steve Perry/illustrated by
Steve Leialoha

#4 SAIL WITH PIRATES
Jim Gasperini/illustrated by John Pierard and Alex Nino

#5 CIVIL WAR SECRET AGENT
Steve Perry/illustrated by Alex Nino

#6 THE RINGS OF SATURN
Arthur Byron Cover/illustrated by Brian Humphrey
and Marc Hempel

#7 ICE AGE EXPLORER
Dougal Dixon/illustrated by Doug Henderson
and Alex Nino

#8 THE MYSTERY OF ATLANTIS
Jim Gasperini/illustrated by Kenneth Smith

#9 WILD WEST RIDER
Stephen Overholser/illustrated by Steve Leialoha

#10 AMERICAN REVOLUTIONARY
Arthur Byron Cover/illustrated by
Walter Martishius and Alex Nino

#11 MISSION TO WORLD WAR II
Susan Nanus and Marc Kornblatt/illustrated by
John Pierard

#12 SEARCH FOR THE NILE
Robert W. Walker/illustrated by José Gonzalez Navaroo

#13 SECRET OF THE ROYAL TREASURE
Carol Gaskin/illustrated by Ernie Colón

#14 BLADE OF THE GUILLOTINE
Arthur Byron Cover/illustrated by Scott Hampton

#15 FLAME OF THE INQUISITION
Marc Kornblatt/illustrated by John Pierard

#16 QUEST FOR THE CITIES OF GOLD
Richard Glatzer/illustrated by José Gonzalez Navaroo

#17 SCOTLAND YARD DETECTIVE
by Seymour V. Reit/illustrated by Charles Vess

#18 SWORD OF CAESAR
Robin and Bruce Stevenson/illustrated by Richard Hescox

#19 DEATH MASK OF PANCHO VILLA
George Guthridge and Carol Gaskin/illustrated by
Kenneth Huey

#20 BOUND FOR AUSTRALIA
Nancy Bailey/illustrated by Julek Heller

#21 CARAVAN TO CHINA
Carol Gaskin/illustrated by José Gonzalez Navaroo

#22 LAST OF THE DINOSAURS
Peter Lerangis/illustrated by Doug Henderson

#23 QUEST FOR KING ARTHUR
Ruth Ashby/illustrated by Scott Caple

#24 WORLD WAR I FLYING ACE
Richard Mueller/illustrated by George Pratt

TIME MACHINE 24

World War I Flying Ace

by Richard Mueller
illustrated by George Pratt

A Byron Preiss Book

BANTAM BOOKS
TORONTO · NEW YORK · LONDON · SYDNEY · AUCKLAND

RL4, IL age 10 and up

WORLD WAR I FLYING ACE
A Bantam Book / June 1988

Special thanks to Judy Gitenstein, Carrie Sorokoff,
Jim Walsh, Robin Stevenson, and Gwendolyn Smith.
Book design by Alex Jay
Cover painting by Steve Fastner
Cover design by Alex Jay
Mechanicals by Mary LeCleir
Typesetting by David E. Seham Associates

Editor: Ruth Ashby

"Time Machine" is a registered trademark
of Byron Preiss Visual Publications, Inc.
Registered in U.S. Patent and Trademark Office.

ISBN 0–553–27231–4

Published simultaneously in the United States and Canada

Bantam Books are published by Bantam Books, a division of Bantam Dou-
bleday Dell Publishing Group, Inc. Its trademark, consisting of the words
"Bantam Books" and the portrayal of a rooster, is Registered in U.S. Patent
and Trademark Office and in other countries. Marca Registrada, Bantam
Books, 666 Fifth Avenue, New York, New York 10103

PRINTED IN THE UNITED STATES OF AMERICA

O   0 9 8 7 6 5 4 3 2 1

ATTENTION TIME TRAVELER!

This book is your time machine. Do not read it through from beginning to end. In a moment you will receive a mission, a special task that will take you to another time period. As you face the dangers of history, the Time Machine will often give you options of where to go or what to do.

This book also contains a Data Bank to tell you about the age you are going to visit. You can use this Data Bank to help you make your choices. Or you can take your chances without reading it. It is up to you to decide.

In the back of this book is a Data File. It contains hints to help you if you are not sure what choice to make. The following symbol appears next to any choices for which there is a hint in the Data File.

To complete your mission as quickly as possible, you may wish to use the Data Bank and the Data File together.

There is one correct end to this Time Machine mission. You must reach it or risk being stranded in time!

THE FOUR RULES OF TIME TRAVEL

As you begin your mission, you must observe the following rules. Time Travelers who do not follow these rules risk being stranded in time.

1.
You must not kill any person or animal.

2.
You must not try to change history. Do not leave anything from the future in the past.

3.
You must not take anybody when you jump in time. Avoid disappearing in a way that scares people or makes them suspicious.

4.
You must follow instructions given to you by the Time Machine. You must choose from the options given to you by the Time Machine.

YOUR MISSION

Your mission is to return to the final year of World War I, meet the man known as the Red Baron, and discover who shot down his plane. To prove that you have succeeded, bring back a photograph of the Red Baron taken on the day of his final flight.

By April of 1918, World War I had dragged on for more than three years. For the first time in history, airplanes were being used as instruments of war. Brightly colored fighter planes of the British Royal Flying Corps and the German Army Air Service fought in broad daylight above the battlefields of France.

Rittmeister Manfred von Richthofen, known as Germany's Red Baron, was the dreaded rival of every British pilot. On April 21, 1918, he was finally shot down over British lines.

Much controversy surrounds the identity of the man who was responsible for putting an end to the Red Baron. To solve this mystery, you will face the constant danger and turmoil of a world war. You'll have to keep your wits about you if you're going to come face-to-face with the Red Baron on his final day of flight.

 To activate the Time Machine, turn the page.

TIME TRAVEL
ACTIVATED.
Stand by for Equipment.

EQUIPMENT

To give you access to the war fronts, you'll wear the clothes of a young European civilian. These will include a topcoat and boots, as protection against the ever-present mud.

Additionally you may choose one of the following to take with you:

1. A small pocket knife
2. Ten matches in a waterproof case

 To begin your mission now, turn to page 1.

 To learn more about the time to which you will be traveling, go on to the next page.

DATA BANK

TIMELINE

June 28, 1914: Archduke Francis Ferdinand is assassinated at Sarajevo. One month later Austria declares war on Serbia.

January 1915: A German plane is shot down with a rifle from another plane, the first aerial "kill."

March 1915: Anthony Fokker develops device to allow a machine gun to fire between the spinning blades of a propeller.

June 7, 1915: First Zeppelin airship shot down by aircraft.

September 17, 1916: Von Richthofen shoots down his first plane.

June 13, 1917: Heaviest daylight bombing raid on London. Heavy casualties are suffered when a London pub is blown up.

April 21, 1918: Von Richthofen shot down and killed. He is given full military honors by the British.

November 11, 1918: Armistice. The war ends.

EUROPE DURING WORLD WAR I

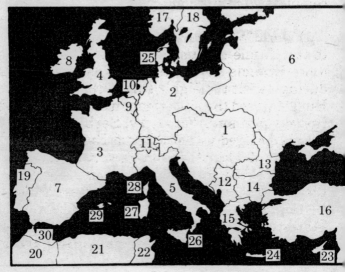

1. Austria-Hungary	16. Turkey
2. Germany	17. Norway
3. France	18. Sweden
4. Great Britain	19. Portugal
5. Italy	20. Morocco (Fr.)
6. Russia	21. Algeria (Fr.)
7. Spain	22. Tunisia (Fr.)
8. Ireland	23. Cyprus (Brtn.)
9. Belgium	24. Crete (Greece)
10. Netherlands/Holland	25. Denmark
11. Switzerland	26. Sicily (Italy)
12. Serbia	27. Sardinia (Italy)
13. Rumania	28. Corsica (Fr.)
14. Bulgaria	29. Balearic Islands (Sp.)
15. Greece	30. Morocco (Sp.)

These facts about World War I will help you to complete your mission.

1) World War I started in 1914, when the heir to the throne of Austria-Hungary, the Archduke Francis Ferdinand, was assassinated during a visit to neighboring Serbia. Austria-Hungary used the assassination as an excuse to invade that small country. Serbia's friend Russia declared war on Austria-Hungary, then Germany declared war on Russia. Other declarations of war soon followed. On one side were the Allies: Serbia, Russia, Belgium, France, Britain, Italy, Rumania, and later the United States; on the other side were the Central Powers: Austria-Hungary, Germany, Bulgaria, and Turkey.

2) While most of the fighting took place in Europe and Asia Minor, World War I was truly a worldwide war. There were land conflicts throughout Africa and China, and naval actions as far away from Europe as Chile and the Falkland Islands. Of course, not all countries declared war at once. The United States was neutral in the beginning and refused to take sides until April of 1917.

3) Throughout the war, civilians were generally treated humanely. However, cruelty was reported on both sides, particularly in Russia and at sea. Hospitals were bombed, harmless merchant ships torpedoed, and their crews massacred. Both sides used spies, and many civilian police forces—particularly those of the

Germans and the Russians—tended to view anything out of the ordinary with suspicion. Innocent people were sometimes mistaken for spies and arrested—and spies were shot.

4) Both sides expected a short war and a quick victory, but the fighting soon bogged down. The armies wound up facing each other over a no-man's-land of barbed wire and mud. For protection the soldiers dug long trenches—deep holes in the earth—and lived in them, coming out only to attack or retreat.

5) Aircraft were divided into three major types. The first were reconnaissance—scouting—planes that would photograph enemy positions or spot for artillery fire. The second were bombers, which would attack with high explosives from the air. The third were fighters, developed later during the war and designed to shoot down enemy aircraft. World War I aircraft were made of an engine, a gas tank, and lacquered fabric over wood. Being in one was like riding a flying bomb. Pilots flew in open cockpits, without parachutes, oxygen, or heated flying suits.

6) Most air fighter dogfights took place over the trench lines. These involved a risk in addition to fire from enemy planes: the fire of anti-aircraft guns from the lines below. Aircraft identification and air gunnery were primitive, and a pilot was just as likely to be hit by his own side's guns as by the enemy's.

7) Engine failure among fighter planes was common, and damaged aircraft were often

brought in for gliding or "dead-stick" landings by their pilots.

8) Manfred von Richthofen entered the German Cadet Corps—a type of military school—as a boy of eleven and studied in the school of Wahlstatt (1903–9) and Lichterfelde (1909–11). In 1911 he joined Uhlan Regiment 1, a cavalry unit that fought on horseback with lances. Von Richthofen served in the German cavalry during the early part of the war. Many fliers came from the cavalry.

9) In the flying services, war still maintained an element of chivalry. It was considered very bad manners to fire at a helpless enemy. This did not stop some pilots from doing so, however.

DATA BANK COMPLETED. TURN THE PAGE TO BEGIN YOUR MISSION.

 Don't forget, when you see this symbol, you can check the Data File in the back of the book for a hint.

ou are standing in a small room in an old wooden house. Through the open windows you see the trees of a forest and flowers growing in the small clearing where the house sits. The heat makes you think it must be summer, but what year is it? And where are you?

Suddenly you hear voices coming from the front of the house. You follow the sound to the living room and discover five kids who look a little older than you. They're huddled near a window and whispering. Hiding behind a partially opened door, you decide to listen in.

"If we shoot the leader's horse, perhaps the others will fall over it," says a skinny blond boy wearing glasses. Some of the other kids laugh.

"We make war on the *Boche,* not on their horses," replies a burly boy in a cloth cap. "Besides, it's *my* gun. *I* say what we shoot."

You don't want to be caught listening in on whatever the kids are doing, so you start to tiptoe back out, but your foot hits a squeaky board. One of the kids jumps up and dashes to the door that is protecting you.

"What do you want?" he asks, clearly shocked to find you in the house.

"I think I'm lost," you answer, trying to smile. The burly boy frowns in return. In one quick motion, he raises the rifle that is clutched in his hands and points it straight at you!

"I think you are a *Boche* spy," he says, pulling back the bolt on the rifle. You hear the sound of the bullet entering the barrel.

"*Boche?*" you stammer. "What's that?"

"*Boche*. Germans," says the skinny boy. "Where are you from, anyway?"

"Shoot the spy," says a girl.

Your trip to World War I looks as if it could end before it even begins! You start to take a step away, but the burly boy grabs you by the arm.

"You're not going anywhere," he says, looking you up and down. Then he turns to the others.

"We can't shoot now. The shot could attract the Germans. Besides," he says, looking right into your eyes, "you *might* be innocent." Then, smiling, he says, "but if you're not, we will shoot you."

All you can do is nod.

"Here they come. Uhlans," one of the girls whispers. Everyone rushes back to the window. Ignored, you creep up behind them to find out what's going on.

A patrol of German cavalry, in gray uniforms with strange, squarish leather helmets,

is riding up the forest path that goes by the window.

The patrol leader is a tall, aristocratic-looking man with a firm jaw and deep brown eyes. He halts the patrol with a hand signal, and two scouts come riding back to him.

"The trail ahead," asks the patrol leader. "Is it clear?"

"It is, Lieutenant von Richthofen," replies one of the scouts. "We saw no sign of the French."

It's von Richthofen! The man you've come to meet! But the von Richthofen you want is a pilot, not a cavalry officer. Before you can figure this out, the burly boy in front of you raises the rifle and aims it at the officer.

"No," whispers the skinny boy, "there're too many." He lunges forward, hitting the rifle, and the shot goes wide and misses von Richthofen. Startled by the noise, von Richthofen raises his sword and points it at the house.

"*Francs-tireurs!* Terrorists! Get them!"

The Uhlans charge toward the house, and the kids scatter in all directions. The boy with the rifle shoves it into your hands as he passes by. You have a good idea of what will happen to you if the Germans find you with it, so you toss it away and scramble out through the back of the house. It is almost the last thing you do.

As you step through the door, you look up and see a German horseman waiting for you.

The grim expression on the soldier's face sends a shiver down your spine. He lifts his arm and starts to swing his saber, but luck is with you. His tall leather hat catches on the top of the doorway and comes down over his eyes.

"Stop!" he yells as you slip by him and get away into the woods. The gunshots and the bullets zipping over your head convince you that now is not the time to meet von Richthofen.

Thirty yards into the woods you hear someone crashing after you. These Germans obviously know the woods better than you do. You'll be caught if you stay here. You'd better get your bearings, fast.

You want to find von Richthofen when he is a pilot. Maybe if you jump to an airfield sometime in the future, you can see him with a plane, not a horse. Or maybe you should stay in the present and find someone who can tell you where you are.

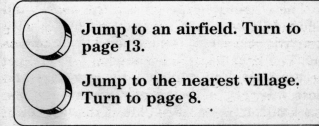

Jump to an airfield. Turn to page 13.

Jump to the nearest village. Turn to page 8.

ou politely decline the girl's offer—you're here to meet von Richthofen, not to shoot at him—and slip out through the back of the café.

Wondering where you should go next, you move off down a narrow alley between two buildings. You can hear your footsteps echoing on the cobblestones. Then you hear another sound, the tramp of boots on stone. Someone is coming! You turn and run—smack into a fat German sergeant as he leads his patrol around the corner. Before you can react, he grabs you.

"So, they're not all hiding," he says. "Come with us," he orders.

Men with rifles step up on either side of you. Clearly, you have no choice. You go along with them.

They take you to the hotel where the Germans have set up their headquarters. The officer in charge—a thin, pale man with cold, fishy eyes—is not at all impressed with your story.

"You were minding your own business, eh?

Very well." He holds out his hand. "Your identity card, quickly!"

"Identity card? We French don't have them," you say, quickly improvising. Amazingly, your bluff works.

The officer calls in the sergeant.

"Take this one home and decide if we have nothing but a harmless peasant here." He favors you with a nasty smile. "If you are not telling the truth you will be shot."

They march you out and back across the cobblestone square. Your mind is racing. You have to get away from the Germans before they find out you've been lying!

Suddenly a German army ambulance comes tearing around a corner and barrels through the square—straight at you and your escort. The soldiers scatter out of the way. Now's your chance! You don't wait for an invitation—you run off behind the ambulance.

Shots tear past you as you duck into an alley, then skid to a stop. There's no way out! It's a dead end! You hear the soldiers coming. Quickly, while you are still alone, you jump.

 Turn to page 13.

You're face-to-face with a strange, hairy creature! Before you can cry out, the creature lowers its head and slams you hard, throwing you back against a wooden wall. *"Urrrruahhh!"* the creature says. You shake your head to clear it and look again.

It's a goat. In fact, you're in a shed with a number of goats. They look at you curiously, as if wondering what sort of animal you might be. You don't smell like a goat. At least not yet. The goat who butted you lowers his head for another shot, so you get up and hurry outside the shed.

You're in a small village at a forest crossroad. It seems very peaceful. Then you realize why—there are no people! You cross the deserted town square and go into a café. There is only a young girl inside, watching you suspiciously from the end of the bar.

"Where are all the people?" you ask her.

"Fool, have you been asleep?" she says. "They're hiding from the Germans. Look."

And as you look out the window you see a long patrol of Uhlan cavalry ride into town. They are followed by infantry in trucks towing field guns, and by ambulances and cook wagons. It looks as if they've come to stay.

"We have been invaded. We are being occupied," the girl whispers. "The Germans attacked all along the French and Belgian borders. At first our army fought, but yesterday they all went away. They said it was a 'strategic withdrawal'. "

"What does that mean?" you ask.

"It means they have lost. But there are some of us who will still fight," she says fiercely. "Come with me."

"Where to?" you ask.

"To the Resistance—the civilian army. We shall fight as soldiers behind the German lines until our soldiers return."

"But you're too young to fight," you say. She looks haughtily at you.

"My father was just a boy when the Germans came to France the last time, in 1870. That time the Germans won. My father fought them then. Now I shall do the same, and this time we shall win."

But you've seen civilians trying to fight the Germans first hand. The last fighters you met nearly got you shot. Still, following the girl may be the best way to get out of the area.

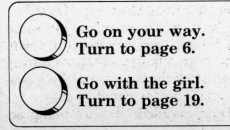

Go on your way.
Turn to page 6.

Go with the girl.
Turn to page 19.

The train starts out for Königsberg. By the time it's in open country, you are dozing uneasily, rocked to sleep by the rhythm of the rails. You are happy to be out of Berlin but are beset with dreams that the men following you are crawling along the sides of the cars like giant spiders, stalking you as you sleep.

Then you awaken with a start and realize that the train has stopped. When you look up, you see a man standing outside the door of your compartment and peering in through the window. He is one of the men who has been following you, and he's pointing a revolver in your direction. Then he holds up a badge.

"Security police," he says. "Make no sudden moves."

Just then the train gives a tremendous lurch, and since he's not holding on with either hand, the policeman loses his footing and tumbles off. As the train starts moving and begins to gather speed, you race to the window and see the two policemen chasing the train. One slips and falls into the ditch by the side

of the track, but the other manages to climb aboard the end of your car. He begins to make his way along the side rails to your compartment.

There is a sudden roar, and you see another train coming on the other track. It's heading for Berlin. If you can jump on to that train, you'll escape before the policeman reaches your compartment. Then again, going back to Berlin may not be the answer. So far you've had no luck in Germany at all.

You draw the blinds. . . .

 Jump to London. Turn to page 26.

 Jump across to the other train. Turn to page 50.

There is a *whoooosh* of sound. A pair of wheels zooms overhead and comes dangerously close to taking your head off. You dive face down into a field of wheat.

Looking up, you see that you were nearly hit by a red plane with black crosses as it took off. You spot another plane in the sky, but this one is red, white, and blue with white stars. Could those be American markings? You wonder.

Suddenly, with a crash of cymbals and a blare of trumpets, the sound of a brass band comes drifting on the air. What in the world could that be? You get up, brush the damp mud from your clothes, and stumble through the wheat field in the direction of the music, all the while keeping your eyes on the two planes.

The red plane streaks upward, with the red, white, and blue one in pursuit. Then the red one drops one wing and dives, rolls into a loop, and comes up on the tail of the red, white, and blue. It's wonderful to watch such graceful flying, but you wonder what's going on. You don't hear any machine guns. And though the planes carry different markings, they seem otherwise identical. Wouldn't planes from enemy countries be of different designs?

You break through the wheat and there before you, you see what appears to be a fair of some sort, with tents, flags, a Ferris wheel, and a grandstand. The flags are American and a banner says: 1922 JOHNSON COUNTY FAIR. No wonder the planes are of identical design—you're at an air show, somewhere in the United States.

You watch as the two planes come in for a landing. The pilots leap out, bow to the applauding crowd, then walk together toward the refreshment stand.

You're obviously not going to find von Richthofen at an American county fair. You turn back toward the wheat field to jump from here, when suddenly someone grabs you roughly by the arm and turns you around.

"What were you doing out in that field?" says the man, a large, unsmiling fellow with a huge mustache. He's wearing a silver star on his coat with the word *sheriff* on it.

"I told you kids to stay away from those aeroplanes," he says. "You could've been killed. You look as if you've fought the Great War yourself, you're so filthy. Well? What have you got to say?"

"I guess I got lost . . ." you begin, rubbing your face. You're surprised when the dirt comes off on your hand.

"What's the problem, Sheriff?"

You and the sheriff turn to see one of the pilots standing there watching you.

"You almost took this kid's head off. I told them to stay out of that wheat field . . ."

But the pilot is smiling. "Look, Sheriff. I can understand a fascination with aeroplanes. I have it myself." He winks at the sheriff, who smiles in spite of his anger. "If you'll just turn this youngster over to me, we'll make sure there's no more trouble."

The sheriff seems happy to be rid of you, and a moment later you and the pilot are walking toward the refreshment stand. He asks you your name and you tell him.

"My name's Douglas Campbell, barnstormer," he says with a grimace. "A circus freak of the New Air Age."

"It looks like fun to me," you say.

"Oh, it is. Dangerous fun. Me, I'm only doing it until I can build up a stake. Then I'm going to start an airline. I think the future of aeroplanes is in carrying passengers. Big planes, with twenty or even thirty passengers—at two hundred miles an hour!"

His enthusiasm is contagious and you smile. You wonder how Douglas Campbell would feel if he knew that someday airplanes would carry hundreds of passengers faster than the speed of sound.

"Hans," he cries. "Come and meet a fellow flying buff."

The other pilot looks at you and smiles.

"This is Hans Bischoff, lately of the German Army Air Service, now just another barnstormer. Hans was there the day they shot down the Red Baron himself."

Great! Maybe Bischoff can tell you more about von Richthofen.

As the pilots lead you over to the food stand, you ask "So, who really shot down the Red Baron?"

"Here we go again," says Bischoff with a laugh.

Campbell turns to you. "It was a Canadian pilot, Captain Roy Brown, flying a Sopwith Camel fighter. Everyone knows that, but Hans can't accept it."

"That's right. No pilot alive could have brought down the Red Baron. He was the best. It was just an accident . . ."

"What kind of accident?" you ask.

Bischoff says that the Red Baron flew too low over a battery of Australian anti-aircraft guns. "It was a lucky shot."

You'll have to get a lot closer than this air show to find out which of the pilots is right, so after finishing your snack you say good-bye to Campbell and Bischoff. You wash your face with water from a nearby drinking fountain and sit down to figure out your next move.

You have to take a picture of von Richthofen, which means you'll need a camera. And you'll need a good reason to get close to the

18

air bases and battlefields where von Richthofen flew. Civilians were not allowed around
the fighting, and a civilian with a camera
could easily be mistaken for a spy. You sigh.
This task is beginning to seem impossible. But
there has to be a way!

Someone has left a newspaper lying on the
bench next to you, and you pick it up. A head-
line catches your eyes: "RIF REBELLION
RAGES, by our war correspondent in Moroc-
co." There are pictures of desert forts and
French Foreign Legionaires. That could be it!
If you get a job as a photographer's assistant
with a reporter covering the war, you may be
able to get close to von Richthofen. But should
you try a German newspaper or a British one?

 **Jump back in time to London,
England, during World War I.
Turn to page 26.**

 **Jump back in time to to Ber-
lin, Germany, during World
War I. Turn to page 22.**

You follow the girl who leads you out the back of the café and down a forest trail. Behind you in the village you hear gunshots.

"Filthy pigs," mutters the French girl. "They will regret this." She seems to be incredibly angry, and you realize that in her place you would probably feel the same way.

Soon you have left the village behind and there are no sounds but those of the forest. The girl tells you that this is the Ardennes. It is so beautiful here that you momentarily forget there's a war on. The girl walks you down a meandering trail, thick with flowers, that leads through the deep woods to a clearing where fifteen or twenty people are gathered around a fire. They are all armed with rifles, pistols, even axes and knives. You, however, have seen the might of the German Army, their cannons and cavalry, and ask what these civilians can accomplish with such pitiful weapons.

"It is not the weapon," says one of the men, a white-haired old fellow, "but the man behind it. I am Old Jacques. Who are you?"

You tell him.

"I'm not familiar with that name," Old Jacques says. "You can't be from around here. Where do you come from?"

"Well . . . I . . . I'm not from around here," you say helplessly. Old Jacques looks at you thoughtfully.

"I did know some people of that name from Sedan. Are you from Sedan? Do you know René Malraux? What is his daughter's name?"

You say nothing. It is plain from their questioning that the Resistance fighters do not believe you, and if you say the wrong thing you could make it worse. But even your silence does you no good.

"This one is a *Boche* spy," one of them says.

Not again! This time you don't wait for them to start the talk about shooting you—you bolt into the woods and dive through a thicket.

 Jump to page 13.

The earth is shaking and a deafening roar fills the air. You clap your hands over your ears. It takes you a moment to realize that you are standing in a long, dark tunnel, and that what you hear is not the earth collapsing but a train passing overhead.

You run toward the light at the end of the tunnel and come out to find yourself on a street. You pause to get your bearings. The walls of the buildings are plastered with painted slogans and recruiting posters for the German army. Trucks, cars, and wagons go thundering by.

You head toward a nearby newsstand and pick up some Berlin newspapers. Armed with their addresses, you inquire for work at several newspaper offices, but they seem to be filled with young German teenagers trying to keep out of combat. With so much older competition hanging around, no one will even talk to you. You'll never get hooked up with a war correspondent this way.

After the third newspaper office, you go to a café to get some lunch. Looking for work has made you hungry. But as you eat, you notice that you are being watched by two men in trench coats. Why would anyone follow you?

They make you nervous, so you dash down the street and try to lose them. You go in and out of several stores, detour down an alley, then cross the street several times. You glance over your shoulder—they've stuck right with you! They must be some sort of German police.

You break into a run and then board a streetcar headed for the Potsdammer Railway Station. So do your followers. But they haven't reckoned on the crowd, and, being smaller, you slip through easily, buy a ticket on the train for Königsberg, and find your car, a second-class-compartment coach. You investigate and find that in compartment coaches the rooms have a door on each side and no central aisle.

Hoping you've managed to give your pursuers the slip, you enter your compartment. Then you cautiously peer out your door. The two men following you enter a compartment at the other end of the same coach!

This is serious trouble. They mean to trail you, possibly all the way to Königsberg. And what then? Maybe you should get off the train and try to lose them again. But now they are in another compartment, and once the train is moving, they won't be able to get near you. Perhaps it's better to stay on the train and slip away in Königsberg.

Stay on the train to Königsberg. Turn to page 10.

Step out the other side of the coach. Turn to page 36.

ou ask the policeman the way to Fleet Street. He directs you to a station of the Underground, London's subway system.

You make your way through the jostling crowd and enter the Underground station just as the walls begin to shake with distant explosions. The people on the platform look up apprehensively.

"German bombers, don't you think?" asks a grubby workman in a cloth cap and coveralls.

"Not bloody likely, mate," his companion says. "Jerry wouldn't dare hit us in the daylight." "Jerry" must mean the Germans, you think.

The train arrives and takes you north, under the Thames River and into the center of London. When at last you come back up to street level, the first thing you see is an anti-aircraft gun set up in a park, the men of its crew standing ready. Without warning they begin firing upward into the cloudy sky, though at what you cannot tell. Other guns begin to fire. The Londoners turn calmly to watch this strange sight.

"Does this happen often?" you ask an army officer standing nearby. He looks at you curiously.

"Not from town, then? No, they usually fire at night. Jerry's getting awfully bold to bomb us in daylight."

You thank him, then ask him where you can find Fleet Street. You follow the officer's directions and find yourself in front of a building with a large sign that reads: The London Times. You start up the stairs to the entrance.

Turn to page 30.

A feather for you, young man." You step out of an alley onto a busy sidewalk in time to see a man in civilian clothes blush bright red as he walks away from a woman handing out white feathers.

As you watch, the woman approaches another young man. The man throws the feather down and stalks away angrily. You notice that some people are crossing the street to avoid the woman. Curious, you go up to her. "Excuse me, ma'am," you say. "What's going on?"

"Those men are young and healthy. They should be in uniform, serving their king and country against the Hun," she says stiffly. "Not skulking around in London, like a bunch of yellow-spined weak sisters!" It sounds as if she's given this speech before.

"But why white feathers?" you ask innocently.

"The white feather is a mark of cowardice. If it was up to me I would have them tarred and feathered," she says fiercely. She spots another young man and goes chasing after him. You wonder if war makes everyone so crazy.

At least now you know that you are in London. It's a frightfully busy place, with cars, trucks, wagons, pedestrians, and streetcars all competing for space. You watch a company of men in uniform come marching by, singing, rifles over their shoulders. The walls are plastered with recruiting posters and signs warning people to conserve food and coal.

But you need to be here. This is where you'll find a job as a photographer's assistant, and that will get you to the front lines and a chance to meet von Richthofen.

You go to a newspaper seller and check the date on the papers. It is June 13, 1917. You pick up a copy of the London *Times* and look through it. The war news is grim. The casualties to the troops fighting in France are horrendous. German Gotha bombers have been bombing the British Channel ports, and their submarines are crippling Britain's merchant fleet. Then, on a back page, you find a story about von Richthofen.

He is called a "knight of the air," and the article indicates that the British, surprisingly, seem to admire the man, even though he is credited with shooting down over fifty Allied planes. Then you find the information you are seeking: the publisher's address. It's on Fleet Street.

"Here now! Either buy that paper or shove off," says the news vendor, as he snatches *The Times* from your hands. You decide against asking him for directions to Fleet Street, but you'll have to find out from someone. You can ask the policeman across the street, or you can go into the pub behind you and try to get directions there.

Ask the policeman.
Turn to page 24.

Go into the pub.
Turn to page 33.

"**C**an I help you?"

A clerk is looking at you from behind a desk in the lobby of the *Times* Building.

"I was hoping to see the man in charge of war correspondents," you say uncertainly. The clerk shakes his head.

"There's no such person, but if you look on the building directory you'll find the various editors and offices. Perhaps that'll be of some help."

You thank him and examine the directory board. The Foreign Section sounds right, so you make your way to the office of the chief of the foreign desk. A man sits behind an office door marked *Mr. Jonathan Shirley*. He doesn't seem very friendly.

"Well, what is it?"

"Excuse me . . ." you begin, but Shirley cuts you off.

"You're taking up my valuable time, and time is money. Get to the point."

"I was hoping to get a job . . ." you say.

"A job?"

"Yes, if there are any openings."

"Do you have any press experience?" he asks, obviously suspecting that you haven't. You don't disappoint him.

"No, not really."

"Have you thought of a career *selling* newspapers?" he asks with a sniff.

"I'd like to take pictures," you say. "I thought you might need photographers . . ."

Shirley raises his eyebrow skeptically. ". . . or photographer's assistants," you add uncomfortably.

"Photography, is it?" He takes down a camera from the shelf. "If you're so good, fix this. It doesn't work. Tell me why."

You're on the spot. You examine the camera, a simple box-type. Then you see that a piece of metal has gotten wedged in under the key on the winder. That could be it. You point it out to Shirley.

"Hmmm, I hadn't noticed that," he says, examining the winder. "Probably a piece of shrapnel. Now then, can you fix it?"

You can free it, *if* you brought a penknife. If not, perhaps you can just open it up and work it loose from the inside.

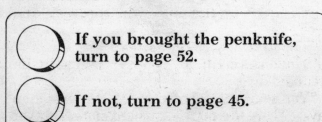

If you brought the penknife, turn to page 52.

If not, turn to page 45.

You go into the pub. It takes a moment for your eyes to adjust to the dimly lit room. Besides the bartender there are only two or three other patrons. One of them is talking loudly about the mismanagement of the war in France, how they "aren't using their aeroplanes the way they should. And Gallipoli! That was a proper mess. Makes you wonder whose side Churchill's on."

"Yeah, well, I suppose you'd do a better job of it," says the bartender. He's obviously heard this sort of story before.

"Well, I could," says the man. "I'd take a couple of those new aeroplane carriers the navy built up into the Baltic, and send a couple squadrons over Berlin. See how the Germans like waking up to mustard gas and phosgene."

The other men look shocked.

"You'd gas civilians?" one of them asks, incredulously.

"You mark my words, mate," the first man says. "There are no civilians anymore. Brother Germany may go to the factory in the morning

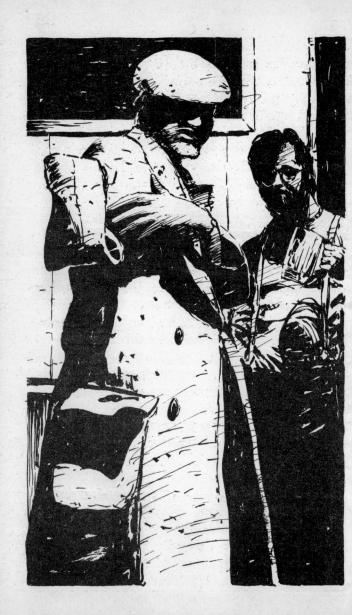

like a proper civilian, but that factory's making guns, submarines, and aeroplanes to kill our boys in France. And gas! So I say give them a taste of their own medicine. Gas them back, I say."

You shudder, then wonder how this man can get away with that kind of talk. How come he isn't in uniform? Then he turns and you see the empty sleeve of his coat. He's lost an arm, probably in the war. If anyone has a right to be bitter, he does.

"And what are you looking at?" he asks.

"I was hoping you could tell me . . ." you start to say. You're stopped by a dull, booming sound.

"Archie," says the man. You look puzzled. "Anti-aircraft guns," he explains. "They's firing at Jerry's planes."

You figure that "Jerry" must mean the Germans, but when his friend says, "Or Zeps," once again you're lost.

Suddenly you hear a high-pitched, rising whistle. Is that a bomb?

 You throw yourself under a table. Turn to page 49.

 You run outside. Turn to page 38.

You slip out the other side of the coach and vanish into the crowd. From behind a marble pillar you watch the two policemen, still in their coach compartment, talking as the train pulls slowly out of the station. You've given them the slip, but it's obvious that without the protection of proper press credentials, Berlin is too dangerous for you. You'll have no luck in finding von Richthofen if you get arrested.

Well, you're safe for the moment. You go to a coffee shop to think things out. Strangely, you find yourself sitting next to a group of Englishmen. In Berlin? It turns out that *they* are newspaper correspondents.

"But England is at war with Germany," you say. "How do you keep from being arrested?"

"It's not easy trying to operate in Germany," one of them tells you, "but we all have Swiss or Danish passports. And there are a thousand ways to get a story out if you don't mind a bit of risk. Still, the Germans watch us like hawks. Now, photography . . ."

"You've got that right," says another. "Even

the mere possession of a camera could land any of us in Spandau Prison for the duration. The Germans are very security-minded."

You tell them that you can use a camera. One of the men gives you his card and tells you to look up his publisher if you're ever in London. "*The Times* can always use a good picture-chaser."

You thank them and excuse yourself to go to the bathroom. There you jump.

 Turn to page 26.

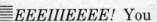*EEEIIIEEEE!* You hear the whistling sound again when you run outside the pub. You turn, ready to throw yourself to the ground, but it is only a whistle being blown by an English policeman.

"Here, now," he says, frowning. "You shouldn't be in there. Into the Underground with you."

"Why?" you ask.

"There's an air raid. Move along."

You sprint across the street and head for the entrance of the London Underground, where crowds of people are heading for safety. As you enter the stairway, there is a tremendous explosion behind you.

You turn to see the pub you were just in burst into flames. It's been hit by a bomb! The people you were talking to are in there. *You* could have been in there, too.

"Keep moving," the policeman says, as he ushers you down the stairs.

There you find a number of other Londoners gathered. They seem to be cheerful, in spite

of the fact that their city is being bombed. Some speculate as to what sort of planes Jerry sent over this time.

"Most likely Hansa-Brandenburgs. Or those big Lohners," says a clergyman. His companion disagrees.

"I don't think so, Vicar. They've got these new ones. Gothas. I read it in *The Times*."

The Times. That's the newspaper you're looking for. And it sounds as if *The Times* is covering the air war. So far, so good.

Then the train comes and carries you north into the city's center.

When you come up to the street again, everyone seems calm, although anti-aircraft guns on the rooftops and in the park are firing, and people are looking up into the clear sky overhead. You look too, but cannot see anything.

"How can the gunners hit what they can't see?" you wonder aloud. An army officer has overheard you.

"They don't have to hit anything. The gunfire is enough to scare the Germans off, and it makes people feel better. As if we're actually hitting back."

"But aren't we?" you ask. "In France? And the Royal Flying Corps . . ."

"Oh?"

"Yes," you say. "They're doing well. I read about it in the paper."

The officer considers this. "I suppose you

could say that." Then he drops his voice, as if he doesn't want to be overheard.

"But I've been in France, you see. In the trenches. It's awful. I'd rather be up there, in the aeroplanes. I'd sooner take my chances with blue sky than with mud."

"But what about getting shot down?"

He smiles. "At least it's quicker than hanging around in the mud, waiting to get shot *up*. If I had my choice, I'd stay in London." And with that he nods and goes on his way.

Maybe so, but you won't find von Richthofen in London. You have to get to the front.

You ask directions, find Fleet Street, and soon find yourself standing in front of the offices of the London *Times*.

 Go in. Turn to page 30.

When you awaken
you are in a bed, alone, in a white room. You
don't appear to be injured, but it's hard to tell.
You are a bit stiff and groggy.

You get out of bed and go to the window.
Below you see a courtyard. From the flagpoles
are flying the flags of England and the Red
Cross, and ambulances are coming and going
through the gate. You must be in a hospital.

Standing at the window you get your first
good look at London. The city stretches as far
as you can see. Some distance away, a number
of smoke plumes rise into the blue sky. Are
they from the bombing? You listen to find out
if the attack is still going on, but you hear
nothing except the sounds of the city. The only
airplanes visible are a trio of little fighters
cruising low over the city.

"Here now. Back to bed with you."

You turn to see a nursing sister standing in
the open doorway.

"You're very lucky to be alive. Most of the
people in the pub were killed outright when
it took a direct hit. The rest were injured. They
found you under a table. It seems to have

saved your life."   She looks disapprovingly at you. "Not that you should have been in a pub in the first place."

"I just went in to ask directions . . ." you begin to say, but she cuts you off.

"Yes, I'm sure you did."

You decide to change the subject.

"It was a bomb, then?" you ask. "From a Zeppelin?"

"No," she says, "Zeppelins only fly at night. Those big bags are much too tempting a target for our gunners. One hit and the hydrogen gas they're filled with explodes like a fireworks display."

You look at her, confused. She smiles.

"No, those were bombers. Nasty, big aeroplanes. But our boys will get them. At any rate, you're not to think of that now. You're still disoriented. We want you to get some rest."

"But I feel fine . . ." you start to say.

She holds up a hand. "You let the doctor decide how you feel. Until then, you just stay in that bed and rest." She turns and goes out.

You sit up and put your feet on the floor. The last thing you want to do is waste time here, you decide as you rummage through the closet and collect your clothing. But when you look out the door, the nursing sister is standing not ten feet away, talking to a doctor. There'll be no getting past her that way. You slip back into your room.

You go to the window. Unfortunately you're on the third floor. Below you is a courtyard used for service deliveries. In the courtyard is a laundry wagon, surrounded by big baskets of dirty linen. Laundrymen are unloading clean linen for the hospital and collecting the dirty laundry. It isn't a fire escape, but it'll have to do. And your timing will have to be perfect.

You open the window wide and ease the door to the corridor open just enough for the nurse to hear. Then, with a terrible crash, you knock over your chair. You wait. She must've heard that. You hear her footsteps in the hall, and then the door to your room begins to open.

 Turn to page 58.

You don't have a penknife, so you pop the camera open to free the winder. A spool of film drops out, unrolling across the desk. Mr. Shirley slams his fist down on the desk and jumps up, his face red with rage.

"That was valuable film!" he cries. "Pictures of the naval engagement at Jutland. And now you've ruined it! Get out of my office! Get out of my sight!"

You scuttle out the door as Shirley scoops up a paperweight and throws it at you. There's no point in trying to apologize. You've certainly blown your chance to be a picture-chaser. Now you'll never get to meet and talk with von Richthofen. But there is a young, redhaired man standing in the hall and laughing. He shakes his head.

"I see you've met the boss, Old Ironhead. Didn't get the job, huh?"

"No. I was going . . . I'm a photographer . . . that is, a photographer's assistant . . ."

"We're short on photographers," the young man says. He laughs again. "Even photographers' assistants. He should have hired you. Come with me."

He takes you to a man named Reaves, who hands you a camera and a leather case full of film. He makes you sign for everything with the warning that anything lost or damaged will come out of your pay.

Trying to keep up with his fast walk, you follow the red-haired man back to the press room.

"But I didn't think I'd be hired."

"I need a photographer," he says. "My name is Roy Ellison-Jones, and I'm hiring you. That is, if you don't mind traveling overseas. We leave tonight, on the Dover train."

That sounds good to you, and you agree immediately. This might be your chance to get a crack at meeting the Red Baron.

That evening you board the train, where you doze until you reach the port of Dover. There you go aboard an old, battered troop transport, the *R.M.S. Minnewaska*, and soon you're steaming out of the harbor.

The ship is running without lights. When you ask Ellison-Jones about this, he tells you the blackout helps hide the ship from German submarines. Submarines? Somewhat nervously, you peer down into the black sea and then out into the night, where you make out the dim forms of the other ships in your convoy and the shepherding destroyers. You spend the next few hours on deck near the lifeboats,

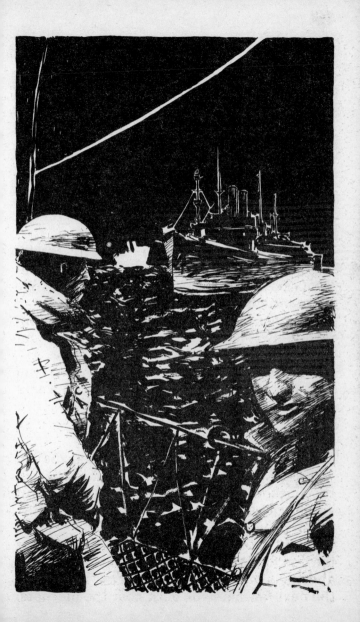

on the lookout for land. But around midnight, when the lights of France are still no closer, you go looking for Ellison-Jones. You find him playing cards with three Royal Flying Corps pilots in the ship's lounge.

"How long before we reach France?" you ask.

The pilots look at each other. Ellison-Jones laughs. "I never said we were going to France. We're bound for Mesopotamia, to cover the campaign against the Turks."

You thank him for telling you and stumble back out to the rail. The Turks! A long voyage and a long way from von Richthofen. Still, you might learn something.

You can stay with the ship and go on to the Middle East. Then again, you can try to find a German airfield on the western front. You remember that the last time you jumped to an airfield, you were five years and five thousand miles off.

 Stay with the ship. Turn to page 55.

 Jump to the western front. Turn to page 69.

Certain that the bombs will be coming through the ceiling at any minute, you throw yourself under the table. Nothing happens. You look up into a face that's looking down at you. It is the one-armed man.

"A bit jumpy, aren't we? That's a bobby whistling, not a bomb. This pub's as safe as houses."

At that moment there is a tremendous explosion, and the shock wave knocks you cold.

Turn to page 42.

You find yourself in the vestibule between two of the cars on the other train. It begins to pick up speed and soon has left the Königsberg train and your pursuers far behind.

Unlike your last ride, this coach has an aisle running through the car. You go to the door of the first compartment and wrench it open to find yourself in the midst of a group of young German officers. They look up from their dinner of bread and sausages.

"What have we here?" one of them says.

"Are you flying officers?" you ask uncertainly, but they laugh.

"No, artillery," says the youngest-looking. He taps the patch on his collar. "Gunners. We are heading for the Balkans, to Salonika."

"We'll drop a few presents on the British, we will," says another. For men heading into combat they seem very cheerful.

Von Richthofen served on the western front, in France. The Balkans, in the eastern part of Europe, are the last place you want to go, so you excuse yourself and go out into the corridor.

There is no one about. Perhaps you should have gone to London in the first place.

Just then the door at one end opens and the conductor comes in. He stares at you. "How did you get on this train?"

It seems you are not welcome. You back away and head for the other end of the car, fast, as you hear shouts behind you, "Stop, you there!"

On the end platform there is a ladder. You grab on and climb up to the roof. You watch as the conductor goes into the next coach looking for you.

So far Germany has been nothing but trouble. Perhaps you should have gone to London in the first place.

 Jump to London. Turn to page 26.

You prod the piece of shrapnel with your penknife, and the stuck winder yields. Mr. Shirley is impressed. He fishes out a scrap of paper and begins writing.

"I like a young person with ingenuity. You take this note down to Mr. Reaves in the equipment department and borrow a camera and film. Then see Mr. Morrow at the French desk. He will arrange for you to be paid."

Reaves, a tall, sharp-eyed individual, makes you sign for each item as he hands it over. At least a half dozen times he says, "If this is lost or damaged it comes out of your salary." Finally you are able to get free of him and find Mr. Morrow.

With your camera in hand, you stand before Mr. Morrow and fidget, waiting to be noticed. He looks up, a tall wispy man with a mustache. "You're the new assistant picture-chaser? You're a bit young, but still, if Shirley approved you, you must know what you're doing."

You're not so sure of that, but Mr. Morrow continues, "Get your kit together. We leave on the Dover train at nine for France."

You spend the afternoon napping in the press room and checking over the gear you've signed out. You eat a light supper at the café next door, then board the train with Morrow and his other assistant, a nervous-looking young man named Dickinsen.

"Are you the photographer?" you ask him. He smiles crookedly.

"No, you are," he says.

"But I thought . . ."

"I'm sure you did. No, the paper's been understaffed since the war started. We're all doing double duty. We can't afford a proper crew, so you've been promoted. You're now an official *Times* photographer."

He favors you with another wry grin. "I trust you're impressed."

"I am," you say. "But what's your job?"

Dickinsen explains that he's to look after the pigeons that will be used to dispatch stories from the front. The paper uses homing pigeons to collect stories from their various correspondents in France and Belgium. The pigeons fly to coops on the roof of the *Times* Building.

"Will the pictures I take also go by pigeon?" you ask.

"No," says Dickinsen. "That would be too chancy. Your photographic film will go by the slower, more reliable French railway system. We can always rewrite the stories, but a picture is 'a frozen moment in time,' or so Mr. Morrow is fond of saying."

"Where are we going, exactly?" you ask Morrow. "I don't know a lot about France."

"We're going to the western front," Morrow answers. "The line across France that the Allies are holding against the Germans. We'll cover this new aerial warfare. Interview the fliers, perhaps slip across the line, get a word with the old Red Baron himself."

You're in luck. This could be your first direct lead to von Richthofen. Perhaps you'll be able to get a picture of him!

"You mean that we might even cross the lines?" you ask. "Go over to the German side?"

"Well, we're not supposed to," Morrow says, smiling. "But they're usually too busy to stop us."

"Who's 'they'?" you ask.

"The men with the guns," he says. "The soldiers, ours and theirs." He glances out the window. "We're coming into Dover. Let's get our gear."

Turn to page 59.

he *Minnewaska* plods along uneventfully, escorted by two destroyers and a lumbering Canadian cruiser. Britain falls behind as you cross the Bay of Biscay and cruise down the coast of the Iberian Peninsula, where the escort is relieved by two Portuguese destroyers. On the morning of the fifth day you sight Gibraltar.

The Rock, as it is called, is a majestic sight, rising through the mists. Ellison-Jones tells you that it's been a British outpost for at least two hundred years.

"The Spanish would like it back, of course," he says, "but there's no chance of that. Not until the apes leave, at any rate."

"What apes?"

He laughs. "Barbary apes. They live on The Rock. They have nests, or caves, or whatever up there. Legend says that Gibraltar will be British as long as there are apes on The Rock. So, as you might guess, we treat the apes very well."

In Gibraltar the *Minnewaska* comes alongside the pier only long enough to take on coal and a deckload of airplanes before resuming her journey. You look at the sleek destroyers and high-sided cruisers in the harbor and ask Ellison-Jones which of them will be your escort.

"None, I'm afraid. Their job is to guard the sea lanes to Britain. Since the Italians have the Austrian Fleet bottled up in their home ports, and the Germans can't get their U-boats this far, the Mediterranean is deemed safe by the admiralty chaps in London. Therefore, we don't need an escort to the Middle East. At least that's what they think."

You don't like the sound of that. "What do *you* think?"

"I think that if the Germans want to operate submarines in the Mediterranean, they'll get them here if they have to send them over the Alps by train."

Apparently Ellison-Jones's opinion is shared by the *Minnewaska*'s captain, because there are twice as many lookouts on duty when the ship leaves that night.

The next morning the ship continues to steam along through the western Mediterranean toward Malta. The day is clear and the sea is calm as you go up to look over the Model RE.8 airplanes on deck. They seem to be made of nothing but wood, wire, and linen, and they look more dangerous to fly in than they would be to any enemy. But this is the part of the war you've come to see.

Suddenly there is a shout from one of the lookouts, who is pointing off to the north. You rush to the rail. Something is streaking through the water toward the ship. What is that? you think, as the ship starts to come about. Then someone cries, "Torpedo!"

It's headed right for you. You decide it's time to jump—but before you can, the deck beneath you explodes, and everything goes black.

 Turn to page 64.

ou are in an alley across from the hospital. You come out and head down the street and past the courtyard where the nursing sister and the laundrymen are searching through the linen baskets for you.

"If anyone'd jumped in there I'd have heard it," protests the wagon driver.

"Just keep looking," says the nursing sister.

Your trick worked. The nurse doesn't realize you jumped in time—she just thinks you jumped out the window!

You decide to keep looking for a newspaper office, and moments later you find a policeman, who directs you to Fleet Street. Half an hour later you are at the offices of the London *Times*.

Turn to page 30.

In Dover you board a transport ship for the brief cruise to France. After debarking at Cherbourg and catching a ride to the station, you board a French train to the front. As you climb down from the crowded troop car you see airplanes fighting in the skies above you.

"This is perfect," says Morrow. "As soon as we check in with the district censor, we're off for the front."

The three of you get a ride up to the lines with a French ambulance. While Morrow goes off to interview pilots, you help Dickinsen set up his pigeon coops. Dickinsen is miserable. He hates the violence and killing of war and wants no part of it, even as an observer.

"Then why did you come?" you ask.

"My father is a colonel in the Seaforth Highlanders, fighting near here. If I didn't at least see it, he'd never forgive me. The family honor is at stake, don't y'know."

After you finish with the coops, Dickensen sits down to write a letter to his mother, and you wander up across the fields toward the trenches. Perhaps you can get a closer look at the action, even see an aerial battle firsthand!

Suddenly a red three-winged fighter plane drops down out of the clouds and, trailing smoke, plummets toward you. You dive into the bushes as the German airplane bounces down onto the field and comes to a stop. A young pilot jumps out, brandishing a revolver. You notice with surprise that the pilot is Hans Bischoff, the young man you met in Kansas! It's odd that he didn't recognize you at the county fair—maybe you were just too dirty.

After making sure that he's alone, Bischoff douses his crippled plane with gasoline and prepares to set it on fire. Still hidden in the bushes, you aim your camera and snap his picture. Then, carefully, so as not to alarm him, you come out of hiding.

"Who are you?" he growls, pointing the pistol at you.

"I'm a reporter," you say, talking fast, trying to distract him from shooting you. "I'm trying to get a story on the war in the air. Can I take your picture?"

He nods, then puts his pistol away.

"I'm sorry I snapped at you. I'm a bit on edge. This is the first time I've been shot down."

You take a picture, then watch as Bischoff sets fire to his plane. You take a picture of the fire as well.

As you do, another red fighter swoops down and lands. Hans runs out to meet it, and you follow him.

It is von Richthofen! You recognize him even though he's wearing his leather flying helmet. You get your camera ready for another shot, as von Richthofen asks Bischoff if he's all right.

"Yes, but I guess I'll be a prisoner," Hans says morosely.

"Nonsense," says the Red Baron, "not if you can hang on to my wing."

"What do you mean?" Hans sounds shocked.

"Just because there's no room for you *in* the plane doesn't mean you can't ride *on* it," the Red Baron says. "Just hold on tight!"

As Hans braces himself, you ask if you can take another picture. Von Richthofen looks puzzled, but Bischoff laughs.

"Just a photographer," he says. "No trouble at all."

"Very well then," von Richthofen says to you. "But hurry."

You do. Then the little plane with its two passengers, one inside the cockpit and one clinging on outside, bounces down the field. Overloaded, it just manages to lift off.

This is the second time you've seen von Richthofen, and you are fascinated by the man. You want to know more about him. You want to know what makes a man become an aerial ace. Perhaps there was something in the way he lived that made his death more than just a statistic.

You decide to look in on other parts of his life, and that gives you a lot of options. You can look for him in the future, or in the past. Or you can meet him at his airfield.

 Seek von Richthofen in the past. Turn to page 81.

 Seek him in the future. Turn to page 115.

 Find his airfield. Turn to page 69.

You seem to be floating on a huge green cloud, up and down, up and down. But you can't breathe.

"Wake up! Wake up, or you'll drown!"

You open your eyes and find them stinging with salt. In surprise you cry out—and immediately swallow a mouthful of seawater.

You're in the water, but someone has an arm about your chest. You cough up some of the seawater you've swallowed. Now you remember. Your ship was torpedoed.

"Keep your mouth closed," says your rescuer. "And don't swallow any salt water. It'll just make you thirsty."

As your eyes clear, you see in the distance the old *Minnewaska* going down, surrounded by a flock of lifeboats. But why aren't we there? you wonder. And who's got me? Your rescuer releases you and turns you around. It's Ellison-Jones.

"Are you all right now? Can you swim?"

"I think so," you reply. "Shall we head for the boats?"

Ellison-Jones shakes his head. "Too far. There's a hatch cover over there. Can you swim for it?"

Still dizzy, you dog-paddle over to the large wooden slab. Ellison-Jones helps you aboard.

"Use your belt and tie yourself on," he says.

As you do, Ellison-Jones forages in the water to see what else he can find in the floating rubble. He comes up with a short wooden pole, some rope, a canvas boat cover, and a wooden cask of water.

"I think we should try to rig a sail," he says, as he passes each item up onto your raft. It seems like an awful lot of work to you.

"Shouldn't we just join the lifeboats?" you ask. "There should be another ship along soon."

"There already is—look!"

As you watch, a submarine rises to the surface near the wreck. Hatches open on the deck and sailors emerge.

"Are they going to rescue us?" you ask.

"I don't think so," he replies. "Watch."

You do. The sailors bring up machine guns and set them up. Then they begin to massacre the survivors in the boats. The sight sickens you, and you have to turn away and shut out the screams of the dying.

"I don't blame you," Ellison-Jones says softly. "Bloody war."

"That isn't war," you say. "That's butchery."

"War *is* butchery," the reporter replies fiercely. "And don't you forget it. Ah, the fog's closing in."

The guns have stopped. You look up and see that you've drifted into a thick, clinging mist. You're safe, at least for the moment.

"Let's get that sail up," says Ellison-Jones.

He rigs a mast from the wooden pole and passes you his penknife so you can cut the canvas into the right shape for a sail.

The fog finally clears and you set about your labors. But just as you get the mast up, you spot an island. A short time later you are rolling in through the surf onto a gray sand beach.

"I say, this is a bit of luck," your companion says. "You head left along the beach, and I'll go this way. This should be Majorca or one of the Balearic Islands. The Spanish are friendly. Whoever of us finds them first will send help for the other."

This is fine with you. You set out along the beach and, around the first headland, see a small port. You go down into the town and report to the local police force.

Apparently very little happens here, because you are suddenly big news. You're shown to a local hotel where you can rest, while the police go out to find Ellison-Jones and bring him in.

You go up to your hotel room and start changing into dry clothing. When you turn out your pockets, you find Ellison-Jones' penknife.

Not having a penknife was a reason you had a problem at *The Times* in the first place. This time it will be different. You jump . . .

Turn to page 52.

There is the screaming whistle of falling shells. You throw yourself on the ground as the blasts begin to tear up the ground around you. Then you look up. There is an airfield about a hundred yards away. There are only two planes on the landing strip and as you watch, one of them rolls down the runway, bounces into the air, and takes off. An explosion rips open the ground where the plane was sitting.

You've found an airfield all right, but it's under attack! A shell hits a fuel tank and blows a ball of fire high into the air. Trucks with men and supplies go tearing off down the road. They're abandoning the air base to the enemy. Then the last plane labors into the air and is gone—just as two shells tear huge craters in the runway behind it.

You'd better get out of here before the next shells begin to fall. With a roar, one lands fifty yards away. The next will be right on you. Jump!

Turn to page 30.

A brisk breeze is blowing salt spray off the ocean. It's a cold, gray afternoon and you're climbing a sand dune covered with beach grass. Ahead you see a small white building with a navigation light atop it. A sign reads: U.S. LIFESAVING SERVICE, KITTY HAWK, NORTH CAROLINA. As you reach the top of the dune you come upon a man in a blue uniform.

"Come to see the flying bicycle?" he asks you.

"The what?"

"The Wright Flyer," he says. "The aeroplane."

He points. There, stretched out along the dunes, is a long, single rail. At the near end perches a fragile-looking construction—the Wright Flyer.

A small crowd is gathered to witness the historic flight. You walk down the other side of the dune to get a closer look.

Two men are checking over the little airplane. It has no seat and no wheels, just a skid for riding on the long rail. But it does have an engine. The two men circle the craft and meet back in front. Then one fishes a coin out of his pocket.

"Heads or tails," you hear him say. His companion says something that is lost in the wind, and then the coin is in the air. The first man catches it, looks at it, and smiles.

"What are they doing?" you whisper to the man in uniform, who has come up behind you.

"Deciding who's going to be the first man to fly it," he says.

You watch as one of the men climbs aboard the plane and the other takes his place at the propeller on the engine.

"They're bicycle builders, Orville and Wilbur Wright, so we've taken to calling their invention the flying bicycle," says the man in uniform.

"You don't think it'll work?"

He shakes his head. "Oh, it'll work. But what good is it? It's too small to carry anything. It's just a toy."

The engine of the plane fires off and starts to come up to speed. The crowd steps back. Someone pulls the block from underneath the skid, and the plane moves down the ramp, faster and faster, with a squadron of children and dogs in pursuit. It begins to wobble uncertainly. You hold your breath.

Then, suddenly, the plane rises into the air. The fragile, awkward contraption becomes as graceful as a bird as it soars over the sand.

You join the crowd in cheering as the first successful powered airplane glides across the dunes and finally comes down for a soft landing.

"Marvelous," the man next to you says, "but just a toy. It'll never come to anything."

You wish you could show this man how wrong he is, but you know that is impossible.

Well, you've seen how airplanes started, but to understand von Richthofen, you should know more about the planes he flew.

 Jump to an aircraft factory in Germany. Turn to page 91.

You find yourself in a peaceful city at the edge of a towering range of mountains. A nearby sign tells you that you are in Zurich, Switzerland. And you recognize the two men coming out of the hotel across the way.

"Good heavens, it's our picture-chaser," says Morrow. "Where have you been all this time?"

You explain that you've been picking up background on von Richthofen. "I actually got to meet him," you say excitedly. But this does not faze the unflappable Mr. Morrow.

"Splendid," he says. "Perhaps we'll do a story on him next, but right now we've got an interview. Hurry along. Dickinsen's been having the devil's own time with that thing. I think he could use your help."

Dickinsen grins sheepishly and holds up his camera, but Morrow is already halfway across the square, and you have to hurry to keep up.

The man he is interviewing, Dickinsen explains, is Vladimir Ulanov, known to the world as Lenin, who is an exile in Switzerland. You follow Morrow and meet Lenin on the patio of a coffee shop.

Lenin, who is wearing a cloth cap and an old but neat suit, is quiet, charming, and intense. He speaks passionately of the new world order he wants to bring about. This is the first time you've really gotten to see Morrow in action. He asks the right questions and gets a good story. Then Lenin, without any provocation, turns and says, "I'll be leaving for Russia very soon. Would you like to come along? Report the truth? The world needs to know the truth."

But Morrow says, "Alas, it would mean my job, or worse, my life. To travel to Russia from here, we'd have to go through the territory of the Central Powers, and my stories are not exactly popular there. Regretfully I shall have to decline—though if my young assistant here wishes to go, I shall not object."

Then you realize that he is pointing at you!

Lenin looks at you and smiles. "Well, would you like to go? You would be under our protection, at least as far as we could manage, and I can guarantee you a good story."

Good story is an understatement. If you go with Lenin, you might get to see the Russian Revolution! But that is not the story you've come for. Von Richthofen is in France, not in Russia.

Go with Lenin. Turn to page 118.

Go back to France. Turn to page 103.

Sure," you say, deciding to go along on the picture-taking flight.

Dickinsen says, "Great! I'll introduce you to Lieutenant Tyson. He'll pilot your plane."

Dickinsen takes you down the flight line to a tent where you meet Tyson, a likable young man. He's shaving in a metal mirror hung from his tent pole—though it doesn't look as if he has much to shave. He can't be much older than Dickinsen, who's only eighteen.

"Your first flight?" Tyson asks.

"Yes, it is," you say.

"Mine too," he says. You panic for a moment before you realize that he's joking. He laughs.

"Got your camera?" You show him.

"Good. Let's go. We'll be taking the Harry Tate." You follow him out to the flight line, where he climbs aboard a battered two-seater biplane, presumably the Harry Tate. Then you see the designation beneath the cockpit: RE. eight. RE. eight—Harry Tate. Sort of a rhyme.

Tyson helps you into the rear cockpit, and you see—gratefully—that there's no machine gun.

"I've got two guns up front," Tyson says, "so I'll do the talking. You just take the pictures."

After a terrifying bounce along the runway and an exhilarating ascent, you're soon flying over the front lines. You can see the trenches below, zigzagging like giant scars across the French countryside. Then Tyson taps you on the shoulder and calls out: "Coming up on Jerry's gun pits. Do get a good picture."

Suddenly Tyson throws the Harry Tate over on one wingtip and spirals into a tight turn. Without warning, the plane noses over into a steep dive. Your stomach feels as if it's still spinning.

"Fun, eh?" he yells over the screaming wind.

"Yes, fun," you reply without enthusiasm, realizing that you're beginning to get airsick. Then, as suddenly as it started, the dive ends and you find yourself skimming over the German lines at a lower altitude.

"We're at five hundred feet," says Tyson. "Get ready. Coming up on the left."

You lean over the side and begin taking pictures. As you do, you notice little points of light coming from the German trenches. It takes you a moment to realize that they're the muzzle flashes of guns. People down there are shooting at you!

But Tyson guns the engine, and you begin climbing away from the front lines. When you reach a safer altitude, Tyson cuts back your speed and calls to you.

"Did you get some pictures?"

"Four or five, I think," you reply.

"Jolly good. Let's go home."

That's fine with you. There are a few pictures left on your roll of film, and you decide to save them.

Suddenly, with a popping sound, the fabric of the plane tears before your eyes. Bullet holes! You duck as a Fokker triplane fighter flashes past you and disappears, diving away. You turn to Tyson and find he's slumped over! There is a hole through his back!

You feel sick. You can't reach the controls of the plane—you're even facing the wrong way. And there's no parachute!

For the moment the plane seems to be flying straight and level, but smoke is starting to come from the engine. It begins to cough and sputter.

Perhaps it's time to jump.

And then a red Fokker drifts into view alongside you. The pilot looks over and removes his goggles. With a shock you realize that it is Hans Bischoff.

He seems just as surprised as you are. Then he salutes you, wings over, and dives away.

So much for that, you decide. Time to get out of here. You stand up and get ready to jump, when the plane gives a lurch and starts down. It throws you backward, and the thrust cracks your head against the edge of the cockpit.

For a second, everything goes black. Then your head clears. You don't pass out, but you feel dizzy. You don't know if you can jump now. The plane seems to be falling levelly. You may be able to ride it down.

 Try to jump in time. Turn to page 103.

 Stay on and ride the plane down. Turn to page 107.

lamplighter goes by, lighting the gas lamps on a cobblestoned street. You wait till he has passed and start down the street in the opposite direction. You're not sure where you are, but you notice that the signs are all in German. It's dusk and there is very little traffic. It's obviously not a Saturday night.

You hear voices. Some teenagers are coming along the sidewalk. You duck into a doorway—you don't want to be seen.

"I'm going to be a mountain climber when I get older," says one boy. The girl with him laughs.

"That's nothing," she says. "I'll be an explorer in the Kamerun."

"I'm going to be a naval officer," says a third. He turns to a boy who hasn't spoken yet. "What about you, Manfred?

Manfred? This might be von Richthofen as a boy!

Manfred looks at his friend but doesn't answer. The kids pass, and you silently fall in behind them. If this is really von Richthofen

you may learn something about his character.
What kind of boy grows up to be a daredevil
flying ace?

Suddenly Manfred turns and points in your
direction.

"You," he says. "Lend me your scarf."

"Me?" you ask, surprised. He laughs.

"Of course. I wouldn't ask my friends. They
know I'm crazy."

You give him the scarf. "I'm going to tie
it up there," he says, pointing. You realize
that he is talking about the top of the church
steeple.

He runs to the church wall and takes a leap
at the drainpipe on the sharply slanting roof,
but he can't quite reach it.

"Give me a leg up," he says. You brace him
up and he's able to get hold of the pipe and
pull himself up.

Manfred climbs from drain to roof, higher
and higher, until he reaches the base of the
steeple. The other kids are silent now. They
didn't bargain on this sort of stunt.

But Manfred has seen the decorative wood-
work on the corners of the steeple, and he goes
up it like a mountain goat. Triumphantly, he
secures the scarf about the lightning rod on
the peak. It waves like a flag.

"He is crazy," one of the girls whispers.

"No, he's not," you mutter. The girl looks at
you, but she says nothing. Manfred is climbing
back down.

"Sorry about your scarf," he says, panting happily, as the other kids close in to pound him on the back and congratulate him. "What's your name?"

You tell him.

"I'll remember," he says, "and someday perhaps I'll pay you back."

The kids turn to leave.

"Wait!" you cry. Manfred stops and looks back at you. "What's *your* name?"

"Manfred von Richthofen," he says. "Remember it. I'm going to be a famous horseman."

The kids hurry away. So that is how von Richthofen wound up in the cavalry, you think. But he did not become the Red Baron until he took to the air and flew.

Being a daredevil is all very well, but it takes more than courage to fly a plane. It's also a technical job, a job that you realize you know nothing about. Perhaps you'd better find out. Maybe you should get a lesson.

 Turn to page 70.

The inn is a three-story wooden building on the edge of town. You can smell the rich odors of cooking and hear the sounds of singing as they come drifting on the air. You go to the doorway and look inside.

Four or five officers are standing about an upright piano. One of them bangs away at a sentimental tune, while they all sing lustily. Two heavyset civilians at a corner table are digging into a plateful of sauerbraten, and the bar is lined with aircraft workers. At this moment the innkeeper looks up, scowls, and comes around the end of the bar.

"What do you want, eh?" he says, his eyes narrowing suspiciously. You didn't expect this sort of reception.

"Why . . . I was hoping to get a meal . . . and a room," you stammer. The innkeeper is not impressed.

"I haven't seen you around here before," he says. "Where are you from? You're too young to be a soldier, or even a worker."

You're exhausted. You haven't had a full night's sleep since you, Morrow, and Dickinsen were on the train. But the belligerent innkeeper doesn't let up.

"You can't answer, can you?" he says, backing you up against the wall. "Why don't you go along then?"

You realize that it's suddenly quiet in the inn. The soldiers have stopped singing, and the other patrons are looking curiously at you. Then one of the soldiers speaks.

"Innkeeper, leave off. I know this person." You look up in surprise and see Hans Bischoff coming toward you. The innkeeper stares at Bischoff and immediately starts fawning over him.

"Oh, sir, if I had known that this was a friend of yours . . . "

Bischoff cuts him off. "Yes, a friend of mine," he says acidly. "My friend will need a meal and a room. Now, I think." In the face of the officer's cold anger, the innkeeper retreats to the kitchen. Bischoff snorts.

"Disgusting man." Then his mood softens. "Come with me. We'll get some food in you and you'll feel better."

Over dinner the two of you speak of flying and of Baron von Richthofen, who is the commanding officer of the Flying Circus, Bischoff's unit.

"Flying Circus?" you ask.

"Oh yes," Bischoff says. "A nickname. It means that we're daredevils. I don't know who first started calling us that. Not von Richthofen, certainly."

"He seems like a remarkable man . . . "

Bischoff nods at you. "Oh yes. Do you know that he is finishing a book? It is called *The Red Baron*."

"It should be popular in Germany," you say. Bischoff laughs.

"It'll be just as popular in Britain. Two English companies are fighting over the rights to publish it. The major is almost as popular over there as he is here."

This seems very strange to you. After all, von Richthofen is in the business of shooting down British planes and pilots.

"But why?"

Bischoff shrugs. "They see us as knights of the air, the last true heroes. After we pass on, war will be nothing but slaughter. There will be no more honor."

Then Bischoff remarks that he is impressed that you are in Germany. "You reporters really get around."

You tell him of your problem: learning firsthand about aircraft. "I was surprised at the secrecy," you say.

"Oh yes," he replies, then drops his voice to a whisper. "We don't want you British to know what we're developing, but don't worry. There's nothing secret about the old E. three I'm picking up. I'm to fly it to a training squadron. No one will object if you see it. In the morning we'll both go down to the plant."

And in the morning, after a good night's sleep and a hearty breakfast, you do. With

Bischoff, you have no trouble getting into the plant, and the young lieutenant shows you around the assembly area. There are other fighter pilots there too, picking out their aircraft, but you two go out to where the E.1s are stored.

The open-topped single-winger looks extremely fragile, but Bischoff assures you that it's quite sturdy. "With a hundred-horsepower engine, she'll do a hundred and forty kilometers with a maximum altitude of thirty-six hundred meters. That's not very fast nowadays, but two years ago she was really something."

"Do the aircraft designs change so fast?" you ask.

"Oh yes. The newest planes fly faster, higher, and are more maneuverable." He pats the engine of the old fighter. "I suppose it will always be that way. But I don't fly this in combat. Look there."

You do. Through an open door sits a graceful three-winged fighter plane, painted a bright red with bold black crosses on the sides. Workmen are installing its machine guns. "That's the DR. 1. That's what we use in the Flying Circus, but I can't show you that one. Now come along, my little British spy," he says jokingly, "before we both get in trouble."

You've gotten a tour of Bischoff's E. 3 and seen the type of plane in which Manfred von Richthofen will meet his death, the DR. 1. There's no more to learn here.

At the gate you thank Hans Bischoff and then start back up the road toward the woods. You wonder about the men von Richthofen flew against. Were the British as concerned with honor as the Germans were? Did either side have the edge in battle because of superior airplanes—or did they meet in equal combat? There's only one way to find out. You'll have to talk to British fighter pilots yourself.

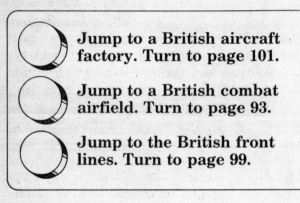

Jump to a British aircraft factory. Turn to page 101.

Jump to a British combat airfield. Turn to page 93.

Jump to the British front lines. Turn to page 99.

reen. All you can see is green.

You are surrounded by green. In fact, you are stuck in a thicket. It looks as if you've made a slight miscalculation. Breaking your way out of the bushes, you discover a busy paved road and, not far down the road, what appears to be a large factory complex covering many acres. Trucks, cars, and men on bicycles and on foot are going to and from it. In the other direction there seems to be only an inn. You head down toward the factory.

FOKKER AIRPLANES, the large sign by the entrance says in German. This is what you've come to see—but how will you get in? There are armed men at the gates and sentries with dogs patrolling the fences. Floodlights are coming on around the buildings. You get close enough to the main gate to see that workers going into the plant have their papers checked, though you notice that when a group of German officers arrive, the sentries merely salute as they go through the gate. Posted all along the fences are signs warning against spying, taking pictures, and trespassing.

How are you supposed to learn anything about airplanes if no one will show them to you or let you in to see them? It looks pretty hopeless.

The stream of traffic coming in and out of the plant has almost stopped. Pretty soon the sentries, with no workers to watch, are going to notice you. That could be difficult.

It's growing dark, and you remember the inn back up the road. Maybe you should walk down there, spend the night, and try to get into the factory in the morning.

 Head for the inn. Turn to page 85.

ou find yourself in the middle of a bizarre scene. It is a beautiful day in the country, and you're on a road running between green fields. The peace of the scene, however, is broken by the condition of the road; it is torn up and muddy, with discarded bits of equipment at the sides. There is even a wrecked truck upside down in the ditch.

A truck comes along, and you flag it down. The truck is full of British soldiers returning from leave and going to the front. You ask if you can hitch a ride with them and an hour later, the truck lets you off at a muddy airfield. You're surrounded by makeshift hangars, tents, trucks, trenches, and dugouts, and a number of small anti-aircraft guns. Lined up in front of the hangars are a flight of small brown fighter planes bearing a red dot inside a white circle inside a blue circle—a British insignia—plus a few old two-seater observation planes. A sign identifies the outfit as NO. 209 SQUADRON, BERTANGLES, FRANCE.

You ask for the headquarters tent, and someone points it out to you. The sentry on guard outside leads you to the squadron executive officer, a lean acerbic major named North.

"Journalist, eh?" says North when you introduce yourself. "I don't like journalists, and if I had my say, you'd be run out of camp—but the colonel says otherwise. That's the chain of command."

You start to thank him for letting you visit, but North waves you off.

"Very well. Look around, talk to anyone you like, but stay out of the way. And clear your story with the War Office censor. Now, get out of my office."

The sentry escorts you out and points you to the airfield. "Take no notice of Major North, mind. He thinks he should be running the war, if you know what I mean."

The man's broad grin is contagious. "I guess you don't believe that," you say. The sentry laughs.

"Let me put it this way. I think both the major and I are right where we belong. You enjoy your visit, now."

You head down toward the airplanes, but little is going on. There are a few skywatchers scanning the heavens for German aircraft, cooks making up the afternoon tea, and a crew of grease-covered mechanics changing the engines on a fighter plane. Everyone else must be asleep or off duty, you guess.

An emaciated-looking captain, sprawled out

in a lawn chair, is reading a book. The poor man looks as if he should have gone on sick leave years ago.

"Hello," you say. He looks up.

"Oh, hello there." He holds up his book. "Victor Hugo," he explains. "Trying to understand a little more about France than I'm seeing."

You introduce yourself and receive a shock when the captain says that his name is Roy Brown. Can this be the same Brown that Bischoff told you about back at the air show, the one who will shoot down von Richthofen? But that can't have happened yet, or the sentry would have mentioned it. So you ask Brown about his health. He is optimistic about his condition.

"I've been ill," he says, "and, try as they do, it's not easy for the people back home to keep us well supplied. We haven't nearly enough doctors, and they're needed much more at the trenches. But I'm a soldier, and a soldier's job is to soldier on."

He prys himself out of his chair and shows you around his plane.

"It's a Sopwith Camel," he explains. "It goes a hundred fifteen miles per hour with an effective ceiling of nineteen thousand feet. Not much, but she's maneuverable and good in the dive. The best thing we can put in the air, and we can only just keep up with the German triplanes."

He shakes his head, then smiles. "Well, nobody guaranteed it would be easy," he says. "But I have eleven victories. Not bad."

He squeezes his eyes shut and wipes the sweat off his brow. "I'd love to chat further," he says, "but I've got a patrol in three hours. I'd better get some rest first."

You watch him toddle off to his tent. Brown—the man Douglas Campbell believed shot down the Red Baron. This could be the day of von Richthofen's final flight! After snapping a picture of Brown's Sopwith Camel, you wander on down to the intelligence hut to find out what maneuvers are scheduled for the afternoon. There you are amazed to meet young Dickinsen coming out. He's in uniform!

He's thrilled to see you. "They drafted me," he exclaims, "so I opted for the Observer Corps. It's not so bad. They taught me how to use a camera, and I don't usually have to shoot at anyone. I've only been shot down once, myself." He grins crookedly. "Silly war, isn't it?"

Then he frowns. "We wondered what happened to you. After you disappeared, we thought you'd been killed."

You explain that you got separated near the front, and this seems good enough for the easygoing Dickinsen. "Morrow's covering the Caporetto front in Italy. I'm sure he's fine. Nothing seems to bother that man. Say, I know what you might enjoy. We've got a picture-taking flight coming up this afternoon,

and the number two observer is in the hospital. You're good with a camera. Why don't you fill in?"

This could get you into the air, but it could also get you shot down—and perhaps killed.

 Fly on the mission. Turn to page 76.

 Don't go. Turn to page 110.

With the *crash* of an exploding shell, you're thrown off your feet. You stay flat and crawl behind some bushes. You lie on the ground, hidden by the bushes, listening to shells and feeling your heart pounding in your chest. When it seems that the shelling has stopped, you take a deep breath and then poke your head up to take a look around.

You are on a battlefield, but strangely enough, there are no trenches. The soldiers you see are standing firm in a tight formation, their rifles forward, bayonets fixed, red coats and white belts gleaming.

Red coats? Nobody dressed like that in World War I! More shells go whistling overhead and you duck again, but you hear a voice bellowing above it all.

"There now, I told you to form a square, not to mill about like sheep. Dress it up, dress it up!"

You get slowly to your feet for a better look. To your surprise, there are red-coated soldiers stretched all the way down the hillside! There are batteries of cannons between the units of troops, and ahead of them squadrons of cavalry are maneuvering. And there, on the crest of the hill, is a small group of officers in bright-colored uniforms.

Another cannon shot flies over you and lands near the officers, but they don't seem to notice. Near you the soldiers are murmuring in their ranks. You hear one of them say, "Good old Duke of Wellington. The plains of blasted Waterloo could blow up around his feet, and he'd stand firm! Nothing scares him."

The man with the loud voice—the man who spoke before—hears him. "You just keep your mouth shut and your ears open, lad," he bellows, "or old· Napoleon over there will have you for breakfast!"

Napoleon? Wellington? You must be at the Battle of Waterloo. You've jumped to the wrong war!

 Jump back to the western front during World War I. Turn to page 103.

The building complex is ablaze with lights and working full steam, even though it is night. You approach the gate to the complex. A sign over the entrance says: A.V. ROE AND CO., LTD. Have you found an airplane factory?

"That you have," a guard tells you when you ask him. "But you can't come in now. The office is only open during the day shift. You'll have to come back then."

You are resigned to finding a place to sleep and having another go at it in the morning when a young man intervenes.

"A picture-chaser, John? Well, I'll show the press around. Come along."

The guard backs off. He seems quite impressed by your host, a tall, gaunt young man who introduces himself. "I'm Tom Hubbard, press officer for A.V. Roe and a cousin of the old man himself. Most of my family is working in the business—cousins, brothers, sisters."

He looks moody. "Here or in the forces, that is. Couldn't make the grade myself. Tuberculosis."

You frown as you realize that medically these are primitive times.

"Yes, I'm used to that reaction," he says, having misread your expression. "Don't worry. I'm not contagious. Here, let's get a look at the line."

It looks much like the assembly area in the Fokker factory in Germany. The only real difference you notice is that here, most of the workers are women. Otherwise British aircraft seem every bit as advanced as those of the Germans. But are the pilots as skilled? you wonder. To meet them you'll have to get back to France. You thank Hubbard and take your leave.

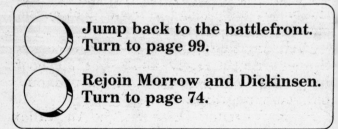

Jump back to the battlefront.
Turn to page 99.

Rejoin Morrow and Dickinsen.
Turn to page 74.

ou are standing up to your ankles in sticky mud. It must be nighttime, you think. Then you see chinks of sunlight coming though the darkness and realize that you are in an underground log dugout.

But where? You wonder if there are other people around. You don't have to wonder for long. Soon you hear, "Ay, don't kid yourself, mate. The only way we'll get out of here's with the bloody angels. If the trench foot doesn't get you, the shell fire will."

"Yeh, too right, mate. I'd rather be back in Sydney with the missus and kids, than shooting Archie here. Johnny Turk was bad, but I tell you mate, this is boring."

Sydney? Archie? These must be Australian anti-aircraft troops—perhaps the same ones that Bischoff claims shot down Baron von Richthofen.

The mud is now creeping up around your shins, so before you sink completely out of sight, you decide to climb out of the dugout and introduce yourself.

"Who're you then?" asks a big soldier with a wide mouthful of bad teeth and a thatch of red hair. The others seem just as curious, but no one is reaching for a gun. You smile and explain that you're a picture-chaser for the London *Times*. That does the trick. Suddenly the soldiers are all smiles.

"Pictures. Can you take a picture to send to my mom?" asks a crusty-looking corporal.

"And me?"

"How about me, then?"

"I'll take all your pictures," you reply, "if you show me around."

You snap shots of the Australian troops posing beside their weapons: high-angled machine guns and light cannons, perched precariously on makeshift stands so they can shoot upward at enemy airplanes. One of the cannons has even been mounted on the back of a truck with wooden beams. It looks very strange.

"Does that thing really work?" you ask the Australians.

"Well," says the gunner in charge, "we're not exactly sure. When there's an air raid we get in the truck and chase them around with it. We hope it'll at least scare them. I can tell you that it sure scares me."

Suddenly cannons and machine guns begin firing a short distance away. "Look!" says one of the gunners. "A dogfight between German Fokker triplanes and our Sopwith Camels." Nearby, a group of planes are engaged in a spectacular aerial battle.

The gunners run to their weapons and begin

firing. The anti-aircraft truck starts up and, with the gunners hanging on for dear life, goes bouncing over the rough ground after the German planes.

You can see tan British fighters and red German Fokker triplanes. In the distance a British plane seems to stop in midair, then goes down, trailing a tail of smoke before crashing with a tremendous explosion on a low hill. There was no parachute.

Then a British fighter—it must be a Sopwith Camel—flies low over your position and fires at a distant Fokker triplane, which turns and swoops past you, low to the ground, with a second Camel in pursuit.

The ground speed of the airplanes is so slow that you are able to get a good look at the pilot of the Fokker. It's von Richthofen!

The Australian gunners hold back for fear of hitting the Camels, and the two planes drop down over a hillock and disappear. But you still don't know whether the Red Baron will be shot down today.

Then the sky is quiet again. The gunners stand down from their guns, and the truck comes back from its pursuit. You take your leave of the Australians and set off to find the airfield the British planes came from.

Turn to page 93.

You hang on as the Harry Tate glides toward the ground. There are no trees visible anywhere, and it looks as if you're going to land safely, as the airplane's wheels bounce once, twice on the ground. Then a wheel hits a pothole full of soft mud, and the plane noses over. You suddenly find yourself flying through the air. You land on your back in the soft trench mud.

You pick yourself up slowly. Well, it could have been worse. You could have landed on your face.

You go back to the Harry Tate. Poor Tyson is dead. With some difficulty you're able to pull him from the plane and lay him out on the grass. Then you retrieve your camera from the cockpit. Remembering what Hans Bischoff did before, you set fire to the plane to prevent its being captured, then make your way away from the wreck.

As you reach the safety of a muddy hillock, anti-aircraft guns begin going off on the other side. You look up and see a red Fokker tri-plane gliding toward you. It's dodging right and left, trying to throw off the Sopwith Camel tailing it. The German pilot is good. He pulls up, and the Sopwith Camel goes shooting past. As it disappears, the German triplane levels off, momentarily out of danger, and banks into a gentle turn. You can see the pilot clearly as he flies slowly by. It's von Richthofen! Suddenly a second Camel drops down on his tail. It's Roy Brown! You'd recognize that emaciated face anywhere.

His bullets tear into the red fighter, and you see von Richthofen jerk forward. He's hit. He seems to rise slightly in his seat. Then he slumps forward.

The Fokker triplane continues on, losing altitude. Brown follows and continues to fire, until the Fokker touches the ground and flips over. Brown pulls back and climbs around in a rising turn, then flies back over the wreck and dips his wings in salute.

So, now you know. It *was* Brown who shot down von Richthofen. But there is still one thing you must do. Jump just a half hour back in time.

 Turn to page 123.

ou decide the British planes look far too fragile to fly in, so you decline Dickinsen's offer. But if Captain Brown is here, then the section of the front lines where von Richthofen was shot down is probably near by.

"Which way to the front?" you ask.

Dickinsen points up over a low range of hills. "It's about two miles that way. Just follow the mud."

You thank him, wish him good luck, and set out, trudging heavily over the uneven, muddy ground. After half an hour, you come to a tangle of barbed wire that looks impassable. Discouraged, you stop to decide what to do next. Then you hear it—a low, rumbling sound that shakes the earth under you.

You look around to get your bearings, but besides you and the barbed wire, there's nothing but mud. Then you see the soldier. He appears to be standing on a ridge some distance away where he's silhouetted against the sky. He doesn't appear to be hostile, so you move toward him. As you do, the rumbling grows louder.

As you climb the ridge toward him, he looks in your direction. He's a British Army officer, and on seeing you he immediately frowns.

"You there. What are you doing out here?"

"Who is it, Captain?" comes a voice from behind the hill. The captain, who had begun to come toward you, stops.

"I don't rightly know, sir," the captain replies, drawing his revolver from its holster. Not wanting to be shot, you hold up your camera.

"I'm from the London *Times*," you stammer.

"You're from where?"

Then several other men appear on the hill behind the captain. One of them, a stocky gentleman in civilian clothing, seems to be in charge. When he asks the captain to put away his revolver, the captain does. The civilian beckons you forward.

He looks at you with great seriousness, though there is a twinkle in his eye that seems to say, "Don't worry. This is all a big misunderstanding."

"So," he says. "You're from *The Times*? The London *Times*?"

"Yes," you reply, holding up the camera.

"Ah, but anyone can purchase . . . or steal a camera. Do you have any credentials?"

"Credentials?"

"Papers?"

You look through your pockets. You were never issued a press card, but you find a scrap of paper in your coat pocket. It is your copy of the receipt from Mr. Reaves, and it states that you have been entrusted with one (1) camera, box-winder type, and twelve (12) rolls of film. You hand it to the man, who examines it and passes it to the captain.

"It seems that our young friend is genuine," he says. "Very well, friend journalist. You may come with us, but no pictures, please."

He turns and heads back over the crest of the hill, the other men following. You follow too. There you see an amazing sight.

The air is rumbling with the sound of growling motors, and you can smell gasoline fumes, but what you find is not an airfield. Stretched out on the muddy fields beyond are twenty-four large metal contraptions, in four rows of six. It takes a moment for you to realize what they are.

"Tanks!" you exclaim.

"Indeed," says the civilian. "There's nothing secret about them anymore, but these are a new type. And we're going to try using them in a new way. A night attack, supported by troops and artillery. We call it combined operations. The brainchild of Captain Liddell-Hart. The officer who almost shot you," he adds.

The captain nods. The civilian looks down at the tanks, where their crews are making last-minute preparations. "Of course, the tanks were my project. I had to fight a lot of

people to get them off the drawing boards."
Then, almost sadly, he adds, "The way this
war has gone, the tank will probably be the
only thing I'll be remembered for."

The stocky, middle-aged man pulls a cigar
out of his coat, lights it, and takes a puff. He
looks at you.

"Nasty habit, smoking," he says. "Like politics. Sometimes I think I should never have
taken up either of them."

Just then an aide runs up. "We're ready to
proceed, Mr. Churchill."

"Very well, I'll be right along." He turns to
you. "Now, stay well out of the way, and enjoy
the show." Then he heads off down the slope.

Churchill. Winston Churchill. You watch
the tanks beginning to move forward and ma-
neuver in squadrons. You realize that this
man, who at this moment seems to think his
career is over, will go on to lead Britain
through World War II. Winston Churchill will
be remembered as one of the greatest men in
the history of England. But right now he can't
see beyond the mud of France.

But neither, for the moment, can you. You
have to get away from these maneuvers to find
von Richthofen. You'll have to jump in time.

Turn to page 69.

An eerie shadow falls across you, and you duck instinctively, but no one's there. You are standing in the shadow of a high wall on the edge of a barren strip of ground. On the other side of the empty strip is a street, and beyond it you see vacant, dead-looking buildings, their blind windows boarded up.

Strangely, the wall behind you seems to pass right through a cemetery. Some of the headstones are backed right up against it. Nearby there is even a large mausoleum with the name ROSENBERG above the door. And a sign on a fragment of the fence proclaims that it is indeed a German military cemetery.

What could have brought you here? you wonder, looking around. The buildings in the distance actually look modern. You decide to examine the gravestones.

Many have the Iron Cross, the standard German military medal, carved into them, though on a few it has been chipped away. Before many of the names you find *Kapitän, Leutnant,* or *Major.* Then you see it: a modest headstone bearing the name, MANFRED V. RICHTHOFEN, and the dates of his life: 1892–1918.

You hadn't meant to come quite this far into the future.

"Stay where you are!" an amplified voice booms out. There are speakers on the wall!

116

You look around. From a concrete guard tower, a soldier is pointing a very lethal, very modern-looking automatic weapon at you.

"Do not move." he orders. "A *Volkspolizei* patrol is on its way. They will bring you in. Stay where you are."

Then you notice that the high wall is studded with barbed wire and spikes. Other wires run through glass insulators—they're electric wires. You should figure out where you are.

You look at the iron sign again. The Cemetery des Invalides, Berlin. Berlin. You've definitely gone too far into the future! You're at the Berlin Wall! And you are in East Berlin!

You take a step away from the tower and the soldier fires. Bullets ricochet around the tombstones. If you can just get to the mausoleum . . .

Two trucks screech to a halt on the road, and troops start pouring out. You'll have to chance it.

You duck and run, bullets bouncing around you, and make it to the safety of the mausoleum doorway. You can hear the soldiers coming toward you as you hide yourself from view.

You can't be seen in the doorway. Unless you wish to become a long-term guest of the East German government, it's time to jump.

 Turn to page 81.

That night there's a soft tapping on the door of your hotel room. It's Lenin. "Are you still willing to go with us?" he asks.

"Yes, of course I am," you answer, yawning and trying not to sound as sleepy as you feel.

"Come on then."

You follow Lenin out into the night and across the square to the train station, where his wife and his supporters are waiting. Several other people have come down to see them off, though you don't see any other reporters.

"This was supposed to be a secret," Lenin murmurs good-naturedly. "Ah well, politics is a public business."

The lot of you board a railway coach coupled to the tail end of a Swiss passenger train. Then the train pulls out, as the well-wishers on the platform wave. Lenin does not seem to notice.

"Are you worried?" you ask.

"Oh yes," he replies. "Making a revolution is a very serious affair. We could all be arrested and shot." He smiles at you.

"Not you, of course. The press is neutral."

You certainly hope so, remembering how little protection it's been so far.

You find out how serious an affair this revolution really is an hour later, when the train reaches the German border and your car is uncoupled, then switched onto the back of a German train. German guards are posted on the platform, and the window shades are nailed shut. The leader of the German escort politely but firmly informs Lenin that if any of his people attempt to communicate with the German people enroute, they will be shot.

"So, they've sealed off the train," one of the men says, amused. "They don't want us infecting the Germans with our revolution."

"Well, we won't," says Lenin. "At least not yet."

"If the Germans are so afraid of you," you ask him, "why are they letting you travel through Germany to get back to Russia?"

"A good question," Lenin replies. "A political question. The Germans believe that if our revolution succeeds, it will knock Russia out of the war. Germany will then be free to concentrate on France and Britain."

It sounds insidious. "Will you take Russia out of the war?" you ask.

Lenin nods. "Of course. This is capitalists' war, rich men's war. The Russian people must concentrate on their own problems at home and not go running off to die for British and French aristocrats."

It sounds confusing to you, so you settle down and wait to see what will happen.

The train rolls through Germany and into Russia, where it is again transferred, this time to a Russian train.

Finally, many weary hours later, it arrives at the Finland Station in Petrograd, Russia's greatest city. There the Bolsheviks, members of Lenin's political faction, are waiting to greet him, and as his party alights, they are bundled into cars and spirited off, to the cheers of crowds of workers. You try to stay with them but are quickly separated by the crowd.

You look around, confused. This is the city that will someday become Leningrad—Lenin's City—and you haven't a clue where anything is. The streets, broad and flanked with imposing stone buildings, seem to be full of angry workers, rebellious army units, and squadrons of armored cars that drive through the streets shooting at anything that moves. You walk for some time until you are thoroughly lost.

You are thinking that it might be a good idea to jump back to England, when you hear a voice: "Hey, you!" A young boy, bundled up against the cold, beckons to you from a doorway.

"You arrived with Lenin," he says, his voice a harsh whisper. "I've been following you from the train station."

"Yes."

"Then come on. I know where he's staying."

122

Grateful for the help, you follow the boy into a large stone building. You notice that both the insignia and name have been pried out of the stones. "That happened during the first uprising," says the boy. "There was a lot of shooting."

You're beginning to get nervous, but you follow him.

"This one," the boy cries, leading you into a room where two strong men grab you.

"Another Bolshevik traitor," one of them cries. "Take him out back to be shot."

"But I'm a reporter," you protest frantically.

"You're too young to be a reporter," one of them says. But the other holds up his hand.

"Perhaps also too young to be shot," he says. "Let's get him a room in the hotel."

That, at least, sounds promising. But the hotel turns out to be a dark and miserable cell in the basement. The two men lock you in and leave, laughing.

You've had enough of Russia. The minute they close the door and leave you alone, you jump.

 Turn to page 26.

You're standing between two airplane hangars. As you turn, you see a German patrol come around the corner. The sergeant levels his rifle at you.

"You there! Halt!" he says. Two other soldiers take you by the arms.

"What have we here, then?" And then the sergeant sees your camera. "*Ach,* a spy!"

He reaches for the camera. After all you've been through, you can't let him have it, so you stamp down on the foot of one of your captors. As he cries out in pain, you slip under the sergeant's reach and run.

"Stop or I'll shoot!" he bellows. You break from between the hangars and sprint across the field. You can hear the soldiers behind you, but when you glance back to see how close they are, you run smack into something.

"Here now, what's this?" says a familiar voice, as hands reach out to steady you. You look up into the face of Manfred von Richthofen. "Don't I know you?" he says.

"It's a spy, sir," the sergeant says as he runs up.

"Nonsense. This is no spy." Hans Bischoff says, stepping into view. "It's all right, sergeant. There's no problem."

Respectful of pilots' authority, the soldiers turn to leave. Around you red triplanes are being readied for takeoff, but you have to be sure what's going on before you take action.

"What day it is?" you ask.

"April twenty-first," says Bischoff. "Why?"

This is von Richthofen's last flight. In a matter of minutes, he'll meet Roy Brown.

"Look, we'd love to stay and chat," von Richthofen says, "but we have a job to do."

"Can I take your picture?" you blurt out. Bischoff shrugs and smiles, and the Red Baron laughs.

"For a friend of Hans, of course."

You step back, focus, and take the picture. Von Richthofen smiles and climbs up into his plane.

"Wait here, and when we come back I'll give you a story."

But you know that's not to be. Von Richthofen guns the engine and waves. The fragile little fighter moves out onto the runway, gathers speed, and lifts off into the cloudy sky. You watch as Manfred von Richthofen flies off to meet his destiny—and disappears into history.

And you have your picture.

MISSION COMPLETED.

DATA FILE

Page 18: The German police tend to view foreigners with suspicion.

Page 23: If they think you're a spy, you could be shot. Is Konigsberg where you want to go?

Page 29: What was the date of that bombing raid? You can check the time line in the Data Bank.

Page 35: Do you really want to stay in this pub? You can check your time line in the Data Bank.

Page 48: Von Richthofen never served in the Middle East.

Page 63: Can you be sure you'll find *his* airfield?

Page 75: Will the Russian Revolution tell you anything about von Richthofen?

Page 80: You don't know where you're jumping to, but you do know where the plane's going.

Page 98: Is it time you found out what flying is like?

About the Contributors

RICHARD MUELLER is the author of *Jernigan's Egg* and *Ghostbusters*. His short fiction has appeared in various magazines and anthologies including *Fantasy and Science Fiction* and *Asimov's*. A former actor, he now lives in Los Angeles where he writes screen- and teleplays.

GEORGE PRATT, working from his studio in New York, spends most of his time working on paintings for galleries. He is currently represented by Grand Central Art Galleries, Inc. in New York, N.Y., Jack Meier Gallery in Houston, Texas, and Driscol-Ashmore Gallery in South Dakota. His work is also in private collections in the United States, England, Canada, and India, and has been exhibited in the Houston Museum of Fine Art. Due to his interest in the First World War and Vietnam, he is currently writing and illustrating a prestige bookshelf format *ENEMY ACE* book for D. C. Comics.

BLAST INTO THE PAST!

TIME MACHINE

Each of these books is a time machine and you are at the controls . . .